Betty Bunny
Wants Everything

WRITTEN BY

Michael B. Kaplan

ILLUSTRATED BY

Stéphane Jorisch

Dial Books for Young Readers   an imprint of Penguin Group (USA) Inc.

For my mom and dad, who gave me everything I **needed**

—M.B.K.

To A., for being the perfect inspiration for Bill

—S.J.

DIAL BOOKS FOR YOUNG READERS • A division of Penguin Young Readers Group

Published by The Penguin Group • Penguin Group (USA) Inc., 375 Hudson Street, New York, NY 10014, U.S.A. • Penguin Group (Canada), 90 Eglinton Avenue East, Suite 700, Toronto, Ontario, Canada M4P 2Y3 (a division of Pearson Penguin Canada Inc.) • Penguin Books Ltd, 80 Strand, London WC2R 0RL, England • Penguin Ireland, 25 St. Stephen's Green, Dublin 2, Ireland (a division of Penguin Books Ltd) • Penguin Group (Australia), 250 Camberwell Road, Camberwell, Victoria 3124, Australia (a division of Pearson Australia Group Pty Ltd) • Penguin Books India Pvt Ltd, 11 Community Centre, Panchsheel Park, New Delhi - 110 017, India • Penguin Group (NZ), 67 Apollo Drive, Rosedale, Auckland 0632, New Zealand (a division of Pearson New Zealand Ltd) • Penguin Books (South Africa) (Pty) Ltd, 24 Sturdee Avenue, Rosebank, Johannesburg 2196, South Africa • Penguin Books Ltd, Registered Offices: 80 Strand, London WC2R 0RL, England

Designed by Jennifer Kelly
Text set in Gararond
Manufactured in China on acid-free paper

10 9 8 7 6 5 4 3 2 1

Library of Congress Cataloging-in-Publication Data
Kaplan, Michael B.
Betty Bunny wants everything / written by Michael B. Kaplan ; illustrated by Stéphane Jorisch.   p. cm.
Summary: Betty Bunny's mother takes her and her siblings to a toy store where each is allowed to pick out one item, but Betty refuses to choose just one and throws a tantrum when she learns the alternative is to get nothing.
ISBN 978-0-8037-3408-1 (hardcover)   [1. Behavior—Fiction. 2. Greed—Fiction. 3. Family life—Fiction. 4. Shopping—Fiction. 5. Rabbits—Fiction.]
I. Jorisch, Stéphane, ill. II. Title.
PZ7.K12942 Bew 2012   [E]—dc22   2011021963

The artwork is rendered on Lanaquarelle watercolor paper in pencil, ink, watercolor, and gouache.

Betty Bunny was a handful.

She knew this because when she was at the mall with her family, strangers came up and told her mother, "Wow! That one's a handful."

Betty Bunny knew that she must be pretty special for complete strangers to say such **nice** things about her.

And she felt very special, shopping at the mall with her mother, brothers, and sister.

"Kids," her mother told them, "as a special treat, we are going to the toy store. You can each pick out one toy for yourself. **Just one.**"

"I am going to get a bow and arrows," said Betty Bunny's brother Henry.

"I'd better get a bow and arrows too," said her sister, Kate, who knew she would soon have to defend herself.

"I'll just take the cash," said her older brother Bill.

Betty Bunny picked out a little stuffed bunny
that looked a lot like her. "I like this," she said.
"Very nice choices," her mother said.

Then Betty Bunny picked out a Fairy Princess doll. "And this," she added. She picked out a Shake and Rattle Music Set, a Techno Monster Figures Pack, and an Ultra Blast Rocket. "And **this**, and **this**, and **this**," she said.

"Betty Bunny," her mother said. "I told you that you could have just one toy."

But Betty Bunny didn't hear her. She was too busy putting more toys into the cart: a Captain Gizmo Detective Kit, a Spin Art Paint Set, and a Slide 'N' Splash Inflatable Pool.

She didn't know what any of these things were or what she might do with them, but she knew that she had to have them. The little bunnies pictured on the boxes looked like they were having the **most fun ever**. Betty Bunny wanted to have the most fun ever.

"This is for ages eight and up," Kate said, pointing to the detective kit.

"This is going to be way too messy," Henry said, pointing to the paint set.

"This is meant for little bunnies who don't cry every time they get wet," Bill said, pointing to the inflatable pool.

But Betty Bunny didn't hear them. She was too busy trying to lift a giant stuffed panda. It was three times bigger than she was, but she finally managed to get it balanced on top of the cart, which was now overflowing with toys.

"Betty Bunny," her mother tried again, "maybe you don't understand. You can't have all these toys."

"Maybe **you** don't understand," Betty Bunny said. "I want all these toys."

"You can't have everything you want," said Kate.

"But I **want** everything I want," Betty Bunny said.

"You can't be so greedy," said Henry.

"Yes I can," said Betty Bunny. And she put five rubber balls into the cart to prove it.

"See?" she said proudly.

"I think you have a little bit of room left, right here," said Bill, pointing to a small space in the cart under the panda's left front leg.

"Thanks," said Betty Bunny as she crammed a yellow dump truck into the space.

"Betty Bunny," her mother tried again, "if we take all these toys home, where will you put them? Your whole bedroom will be filled up with **nothing but toys**."

Betty Bunny thought about what it would be like to live in a room filled up with nothing but toys.

The thought made her very happy. She picked up a one-thousand-piece jigsaw puzzle and tossed it onto the giant panda's belly. It was so much fun that she tossed more toys onto the panda's belly. And more. **And more.**

Henry said, "You better listen to Mommy."

Kate said, "Mommy is very smart and she knows what's best."

Bill said, "Keep acting crazy. It makes the rest of us look good."

Betty Bunny's mother said that if Betty Bunny couldn't pick out just one toy, then she would get no toys.

She paid for bows and arrows for Henry and Kate, and she gave Bill his cash. Then she scooped Betty Bunny up and started to walk out of the store.

Betty Bunny saw the cart filled with her new toys as they walked away, leaving it behind. She started to cry. Then she started to scream. Then she started to kick her legs wildly.

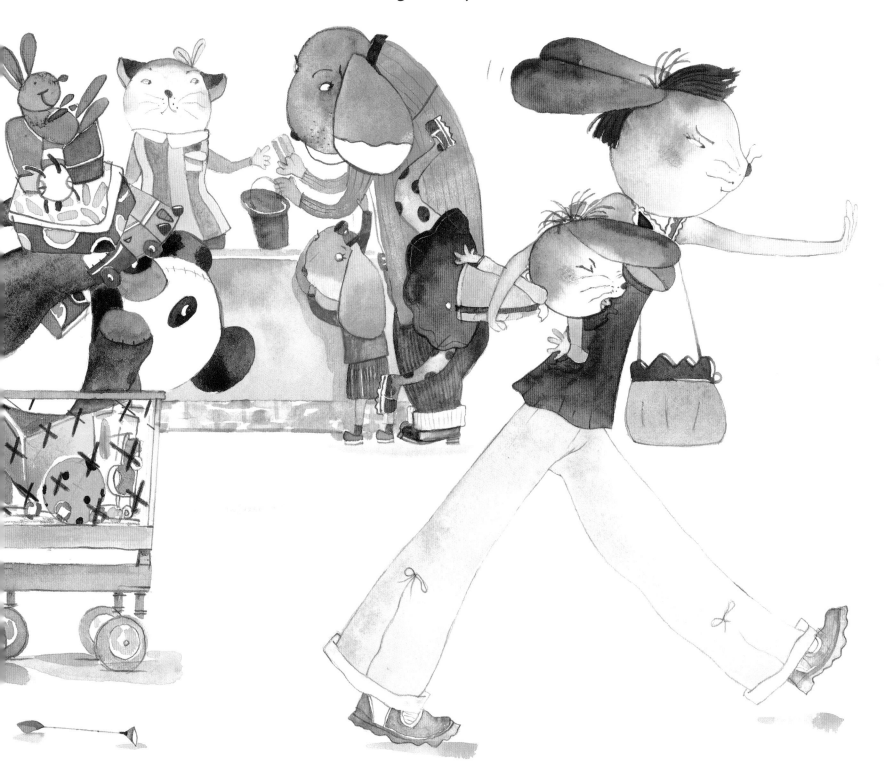

She cried all the way home.

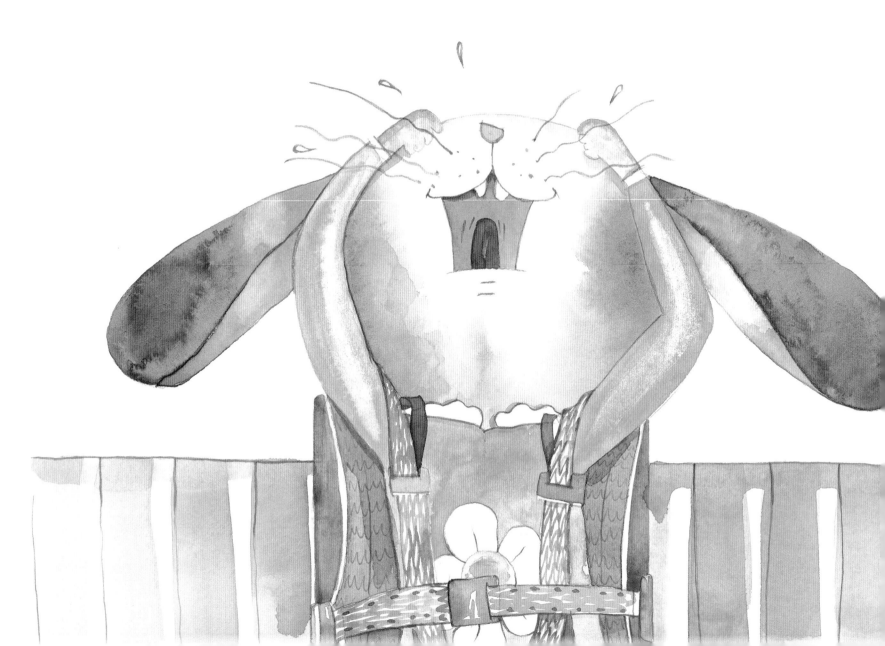

And she was still crying when her father came home from work. "What's the matter with my little bunny?" he asked.

"I have the **meanest mommy** in the whole world," Betty Bunny answered. And she explained all about how she had picked out a few very nice toys at the toy store, and her mean, horrible, **yucky** mommy wouldn't let her have them.

Betty Bunny watched as her father walked over and talked to her mother. Betty Bunny hoped that her father was saying: "Stop being so mean and horrible and yucky and give my little bunny all the toys she wants." She tried to listen to what he was saying, but it was hard to hear over the sound of her crying.
And she was afraid that if she stopped crying,
they would forget how much she
really,
  really
   wanted
  those
  toys.

Finally, her mother and father walked over to her. They were smiling. Betty Bunny stopped crying. Her father said, "Betty Bunny, we have an idea." Betty Bunny started crying again. "I don't want an idea," she said through her tears. "I want toys."

So her mother and father showed her the idea.
The whole family went back to the toy store.

Betty Bunny's mother gave her some money. "This is your money," she said. "You can spend it on whatever toys you want, but when you run out of money, you can't get any more."

Her father explained, "It will help you understand why you can't have everything you want."

Betty Bunny looked at her new money. She liked it very much.

"But if I use my money to buy toys," she said, "then I won't have my money anymore."

"That's the way money works," said Henry.

"You could use some of the money and save some of the money," Kate suggested.

"You could just give all the money to me, then you won't have to worry about this very tricky problem," Bill said.

Betty Bunny made a decision. She saved some of the money, and used the rest to buy the little stuffed bunny that looked a lot like her. "I'm going to name her **Little Betty**," she said.

Her father went to stand in line so that Betty Bunny could pay for Little Betty.

Betty Bunny got out a shopping cart and started to fill it with toys. She put in the Shake and Rattle Music Set, the Techno Monster Figures Pack, and the Ultra Blast Rocket. She put in the Captain Gizmo Detective Kit, the Spin Art Paint Set, and the Slide 'N' Splash Inflatable Pool.

As she was about to put in the giant stuffed panda, her mother said, "What are you doing? I thought you understood that you can't have everything."

"Oh, they're not for me," Betty Bunny said. "Little Betty wants them. And I can't get her to understand that it's just **too much**. Maybe you can give her some money too."